1

I0456577

Happenstance

EIGHT SHORT PLAYS ABOUT LUCK,
OR ONE EIGHT-PART PLAY IN VIGNETTES

by Lowery Christopher Collins

Happenstance

EIGHT SHORT PLAYS ABOUT LUCK, OR ONE EIGHT-PART PLAY IN VIGNETTES

BY LOWERY CHRISTOPHER COLLINS

HAPPENSTANCE,
EIGHT SHORT PLAYS ABOUT LUCK, OR ONE EIGHT-PART PLAY IN
VIGNETTES

Written by Lowery Christopher Collins

Ponderlake Publishing: www.ponderlake.com

Playwright and/or Royalty Information: www.ChristopherCollinsOnline.com

ISBN 978-0-9992241-5-1

These EIGHT short plays may be produced individually, in which case they would be entitled "Happenstance" followed by a colon (:) and then the name of the short play—for instance, "Happenstance: Lucky in Love."

Or they may be produced as the entire series of eight plays, in the order in which they are presented in this script, and called "Happenstance."

HAPPENSTANCE

EIGHT SHORT PLAYS ABOUT LUCK,
<u>OR</u> ONE EIGHT-PART PLAY IN VIGNETTES
by Lowery Christopher Collins

CHARACTER LIST(S)

Short Play One/Scene One— "Lucky in Love" Anna Brady	Short Play Five/Scene Five – "Luck of the Ire" Keenan Larry Milo Nova Otis
Short Play Two/Scene Two— "Lucked Out" Cole Deet	Short Play 6/Scene 6— "Luck and War" Peter Quin Rachel Savannah
Short Play Three/Scene Three— "The Lucky Dozen" Eleanor Felisha Grant	Short Play 7/Scene 7— "As Luck Would Have It" Terry Usha Vincent Wayne Xavier
Short Play Four/Scene Four— "Lucky Strike" Heidi Isabel Jackie	Short Play 8/Scene 8— "Luck of the Draw" Yvette Zed Anna Brady

HAPPENSTANCE

EIGHT SHORT PLAYS ABOUT LUCK,
OR ONE EIGHT-PART PLAY IN VIGNETTES

by Lowery Christopher Collins

Short Play 1/Scene 1— "Lucky in Love"

Short Play 2/Scene 2— "Lucked Out"

Short Play 3/Scene 3— "The Lucky Dozen"

Short Play 4/Scene 4— "Lucky Strike"

Short Play 5/Scene 5 – "Luck of the Ire"

Short Play 6/Scene 6— "Luck and War"

Short Play 7/Scene 7— "As Luck Would Have It"

Short Play 8/Scene 8— "Luck of the Draw"

Short Play 1/Scene 1—
Lucky in Love

Anna stands DR. She faces the audience. As she speaks, it becomes obvious that she is practicing this speech in front of a mirror. During the course of the monologue, she can check her hair or eyebrows as if making sure they look "right." She is sure of herself and careful about her appearance.

ANNA.   I'm your "best" friend. I look out for you. I care about you so much that I'm honest with you about everything. And have to tell you . . . the truth. I know that you and I have been through a lot together. We've known each other a very long time. And I know you think that what we have is more than, well, friendship. Hear me out. Please. I love you very much—as a . . . friend. I can't imagine living this life without you, but (*long pause*) I'm not interested in you in *that* way. I don't want you to be mad. I don't want you to be sad. My intent is not to hurt your feelings. I just can't live my life unless I'm living it truthfully. And no, before you ask, there isn't anyone else. There just isn't an "us." I want us to remain friends. But just know that you and I can't be . . . together in that way. (*Breaking the mood, moving away from the mirror, and talking to herself now.*) That's it, Anna. That's how you have to say it. He can handle it. He has to.

Brady walks in. He is upbeat.

BRADY.   Hey, how are you?

ANNA.   Brady.

BRADY.   What are you up to?

ANNA.   Little of this. Little of that.

BRADY.   That's not your sort of answer.

ANNA.   And that's not your sort of response. (*Quickly adding*) Why are you so happy?

BRADY.   Happy? Me?

ANNA.   Yes, you. Did someone slip something into your drink?

BRADY.   (*Laughing*) No, of course not. Can't a guy be happy? Can't he be glad to be alive?

ANNA.   Okay. This is scaring me.

BRADY.   (*Scoffs*) Scary? Nah. It's just a good day.

ANNA.   Okay.

BRADY.   An important day.

ANNA.   In what way?

BRADY.   (*Containing his excitement*) Anna, we need to talk.

ANNA.   (*A bit somber*) We do, Brady.

BRADY.   Oh, really? Good news?

ANNA.   I don't think it's really news. It's more that we just . . . need to . . . talk.

14

BRADY. Okay. What's up? Is something wrong?

ANNA. Well. First, why exactly are you so happy? What's going on?

BRADY. *(Smiles)* There's just something I need to tell you, ask you.

ANNA. Oh, Brady. You're going to make this much more difficult?

BRADY. What? What are you talking about? What's difficult?

ANNA. It's just that I need you to know that . . .

BRADY. What?

ANNA. Brady, look. We've been friends for a long time.

BRADY. *(Smiling)* We sure have. A long time.

ANNA. And really more than friends, best of friends.

BRADY. Yes, Anna. Best of friends.

ANNA. We've seen each other through of a lot of tough times.

BRADY. Lots of them. Best of friends.

ANNA. And I think we're to a point in our friendship that we need to discuss something very important.

BRADY. I couldn't agree more. We are to that point. That's something I want to talk with you about.

ANNA. That's what I thought. Brady, we just need to think about where we, you and I, are. You know . . . we . . . Whew. I have to get through this. You know I was thinking just before you came in how I can't really imagine life without you.

BRADY. Anna, I couldn't agree more. Yes.

ANNA. Brady. Please. Let me finish.

BRADY. Okay. Go ahead.

ANNA. I . . . you and I . . . can't . . . we can't just . . . Brady, what do you have to say?

BRADY. About what?

ANNA. Why did you come in here all happy? What did you come in here to say?

BRADY. I'm here, listening to you. You asked me to listen to you.

ANNA. But I want to know what you're so happy about. I'll tell you my thoughts in a bit.

BRADY.   Are you sure?

ANNA.   Brady, I am. Tell me.

BRADY.   *(Leaning forward, truly excited to share)* Okay. Anna, I have a lot to say. Promise you'll hear me out before you say anything.

ANNA.   Brady. Don't . . .

BRADY.   I'm serious, Anna. Sometimes, you don't hear me out before you stop me. Please, hear me all the way out before you say anything. We've been friends for a long time, and I think I deserve a hearing.

ANNA.   Okay, Brady. Okay. Talk. Speak your mind.

BRADY.   All the way through?

ANNA.   *(Sighs)* All the way through. Go.

BRADY.   *(Sighs deeply, then smiles)* Okay. Okay. Anna, you're my best friend. You're the best thing that's ever happened to me. We've been through a lot together. It feels like most of my life. What we have is more than friendship, and you know it. I love you. I love you, Anna. And like you said, I can't imagine my life without you. And I don't know about you, but when two people care for each other, when there's love, when there's a history, when it's all just right, I think it means one thing. And it's something that I should have pushed a long time ago. Anna, I love you. I love you more than I love anyone. And, wow, this is something I've thought about for a long time . . .

ANNA.   Brady . . .

BRADY.   Let me finish.

ANNA.   Okay.

BRADY.   Anna, I love you, and I want you to be my wife.

ANNA.   Brady . . .

BRADY.   Anna, you promised me that you'd let me finish.

ANNA.   There's more?

BRADY.   Please let me finish.

ANNA.   *(Deep breath)* Finish.

BRADY.   I know what you're thinking. It's not the time. I'm not financially secure enough to ask you to marry me. But the fact of the matter is that time waits for no man. You can't wait around for the right time to do the right thing. You have to do the

ANNA.

BRADY.

right thing, and it'll be the right time. Okay. That made sense in my head. But anyway . . .

ANNA.   Brady . . .

BRADY.   *(Ignoring her interruption)* Now IS the right time. And this is the right thing. And you know how I know this? There's a reason why I know it's the right time. I've wanted to ask you to marry me for a long time. And money's always stood in my way. Money's stood in the way of many things in my life. Isn't that the way it is for most people? Anyway, I decided that enough was enough, that I couldn't wait any longer, that I was going to pour my heart and soul out to you, that I had to ask you, no matter what—because you know, Anna, I love you. I love you with all my heart. But something crazy happened.

ANNA.   Brady . . .

BRADY.   Something crazy happened, Anna. And it proved it was the right time. I decided last night that I was going to ask you today—and that the one thing that was holding me back, the fact that I'm not quite as secure as I wanted to be, couldn't hold me back from asking the woman of my dreams to marry me. I made up my mind that I'd find a way to overcome that obstacle. But, Anna, having that courage, making that decision . . . Well, I don't have to overcome it. This morning I got a phone call from a lawyer in North Dakota. The first thing I thought was "North Dakota"? Why North Dakota? I hadn't been there since I was a kid, when we visited my mom's Uncle Jack. That was years ago. And I still don't believe this, but this lawyer, this Mr. Masters, well, he told me something that I still don't know if I can believe. Anna, Uncle Jack passed away three weeks ago, and he left me all the mineral rights on a big piece of property that's being producing oil for years. Anna, Masters told me I'm the sole heir to an estate that's worth at least $8 million and growing every day. Anna, Anna, money's not an issue anymore. I'm rich. We're rich. If you'll marry me. Will you?

ANNA.   *(in total shock)* What?

BRADY.   Anna, will you marry me?

ANNA.   Brady, this is all a bit overwhelming. What? Wow.

BRADY.   Anna, I love you. Will you marry me?

ANNA.   Uh, . . . yes. Yes, I will.

BRADY.   *(Grabbing her and hugging her)* Anna, you've made me the happiest person on the planet. I love you so much.

ANNA.   So . . . much.

BRADY.   Are you okay?

ANNA.   Yes, yes, I'm fine. Yes. Brady, wow. Yes, I'll gladly marry you.

BRADY.   I love you so much.

ANNA.   I love you, too.

BRADY.   I'm the luckiest man on earth. I'm the luckiest man on the earth.

Short Play 2/Scene 2—
Lucked Out

COLE enters his house and turns on the lights. It's obvious that he has been out, possibly with friends. It's late, and he is tired. As he puts down a bag or briefcase and his keys, he hums to himself. He finally turns on a lamp that allows him to notice a man sitting in a chair.

COLE. Whoa! Who are you? What are you doing in my house?

DEET. Why don't you have a seat?

COLE. What? I said, "Who ARE you?"

DEET is silent, looks calmly at COLE.

COLE. What are you doing in my house? I'm calling the cops.

DEET. That's not a wise choice.

COLE. What? Who are you? How did you get in here?

DEET. That's immaterial.

COLE. Immaterial?

DEET. Immaterial. It means, "unimportant under the circumstances; irrelevant."

COLE. I *know* what it means. It's just not true.

DEET. It's remarkably true.

COLE. Who *are* you?

DEET. It's more important that I know who you are.

COLE. Who exactly am I?

DEET. Now, you're asking the right question.

COLE. And who are you?

DEET. One step backward.

COLE. That's it. It's 911 time.

DEET. Do you want me to talk with the police about you and what you've done?

COLE. I . . .

DEET. Ah, there we go. The struck nerve. And now you sit. (Waits.) And now you sit.

COLE sits slowly.

19

DEET.   See, I always get the right house. We have a problem. And it needs to be solved.

COLE.   A problem? Who are you?

DEET.   You can call me Mr. Deet.

COLE.   Deet?

DEET.   Deet. And if you think hard enough, you'll know who I am.

COLE.   I'm thinking as hard as I can, and I can't for the life me figure out who you could be.

DEET.   Yet, you are sitting down here at my request--in your house. And you haven't called the authorities.

COLE.   Because I don't know who or why . . .

DEET.   But you do. You may not know who, but you know why.

COLE.   You know?

DEET.   Before you say much more, you need to think carefully about what you want to say.

COLE.   Now you're threatening me?

DEET.   I'm being realistic. I'm a businessman. And you're in my business.

COLE.   I'm a car salesman.

DEET.   Oh, is that your day job?

COLE.   That's my only job.

DEET.   Nice. That's fine. Just think carefully—like I said.

COLE.   I think you . . .

DEET.   I know what you did.

COLE.   *(Pause. Frightened.)* What?

DEET.   I know. I found out.

COLE.   Found out?

DEET.   You thought you wouldn't be discovered. You thought you'd kept it hidden.

COLE.   I . . . what? No. I thought I . . . Oh, oh, oh.

DEET.   You can't expect to keep things in the cover of darkness. We find out.

COLE.   We? What are you? The police?

DEET.   Nice try. I must say that I didn't expect you to be so persistent.

COLE.   Who is WE? What did you . . . ? How did you . . . ?

DEET.   We have networks. Surely you know that.

COLE.   Networks? It was so long ago. I didn't tell a soul. I've kept it to myself for two years.

DEET.   Two years? You did this two years ago, too? I'm here about the recent transgression. Well, well, perhaps I need to take you to see the boss.

COLE.   Recent? It was two years ago. I didn't know what to do. I didn't see her. It was almost dark. I was looking at my radio. I didn't notice the reflectors. I hit her before I knew it. And I panicked. I was a mile away before I started breathing again. I should have gone back. I should have. I did check. She recovered. She wasn't hurt badly at all. She was back at school within two weeks. I've worried sick about her and have been so angry at my own cowardice. I don't know. And I don't know how you know this. And after two years. And recent? I haven't done anything recent, Mr. Deet. I've lived as a model citizen for two full years.

DEET.   A bicycle? A girl on a bicycle?

COLE.   But she's perfectly okay. She was more scared than anything. And I've kept up with . . . Wait a minute. You're not . . .

DEET.   I don't know what game you're playing, Mr. Apton, but I'm not going to play it with you. You've stolen some of the product you're handling for the boss, and he's very unhappy with you.

COLE.   Apton?

DEET.   Yes.

COLE.   You just called me Apton.

DEET.   That's your name, Mr. Apton. Don't play games.

COLE.   Robert Apton?

DEET.   Yes, Robert M. Apton.

COLE.   I'm Cole F. Fulton.

DEET.   What?

COLE.   Look. *(Pulling out identification)* My name is Cole Franklin Fulton. Look.

DEET reluctantly looks at the ID.

COLE.   716 West Harper Drive. Robert Apton lives in the *other* yellow house trimmed in black—at the *other* end of this road, at *617* West Harper Drive.

DEET.   Is this some sort of . . .

COLE.   Cole. Franklin. Fulton. And I've never sold anything for your boss. I sell cars.

DEET.   But . . .

COLE.   And you thought . . . I thought you were here to . . .

DEET.   I still know what you did.

COLE.   Now! (*(Frustrated with himself)* I can't believe this. I'm going to call the cops.

DEET.   You can't. I know about the bicycle.

COLE.   Go! Just go! Get out.

DEET.   It's not that simple now.

COLE.   Look. I don't care. I don't care who you are. I don't care what beef you have with Apton. In fact, I can't stand him anyway. Go threaten him. He deserves it. He's a creep and a jerk and no good. Get your money from him. Just don't tell a soul about the bike.

DEET.   Mr. Fulton . . .

COLE.   Go take care of Apton. You have my blessing. I never saw you.

DEET.   Mr. Fulton . . .

COLE.   And you don't know about the bicycle. Period.

DEET stands and stares at COLE.

DEET.   I didn't look at the house numbers right. I'm capable of making a mistake every once in a while.

COLE.   It's all right. It happens.

DEET.   And you didn't see me?

COLE.   And you didn't hear me?

DEET & COLE.   Deal.

DEET starts to leave.

DEET.   You lucked out.

COLE.   You did, too.

Deet walks out. Cole collapses on his couch/chair.

Short Play 3/Scene 3—
The Lucky Dozen

ELEANOR is sitting, crocheting. Her sister, FELISHA, rushes in. She is in a panic.

ELEANOR.   Are you all right?

FELISHA.   Oh, Eleanor!

ELEANOR.   What is it?

FELISHA.   Oh, Eleanor!

ELEANOR.   What is it?

FELISHA.   Oh, Eleanor.

ELEANOR.   Felisha, this conversation is going nowhere. What's wrong?

FELISHA.   I've . . . I've . . . seen her. Eleanor, I've seen her!

ELEANOR.   Who, Felisha?

FELISHA.   Who do you think?

ELEANOR.   The housekeeper? She's been here all afternoon.

FELISHA.   Not the housekeeper! Mother! I've seen Mother, Eleanor.

ELEANOR.   Oh, Felisha.

FELISHA.   Don't "Oh, Felisha" me. I know what I've seen. I know whom I've seen.

ELEANOR.   Whom you *want* to see! Felisha, Mother has been dead for thirty years.

FELISHA.   Don't say that word!

ELEANOR.   What word?

FELISHA.   Dead. It seems so permanent, so cruel.

ELEANOR.   It *is* permanent. She's gone, Felisha. She has been for a long time, and you still, still haven't let go.

FELISHA.   What am I supposed to do? Go on like she never lived?

ELEANOR.   Felisha, it's been over thirty years. You can't spend every day processing something that happened that long ago. After a few years, after a few decades, it's time to take a breath and move on.

FELISHA.   It seems like yesterday.

ELEANOR. Because you're making yesterday the same *today* over and over.

FELISHA. Why are you so cruel to me?

ELEANOR. I'm trying to save your life. You're my little sister. All we have is each other.

FELISHA. Eleanor, I'm may be many things, but I am not a liar. I saw Mother again. There's not a doubt in my mind. She was wearing her favorite dress, the one we have in storage in the attic. She was even wearing the huge hat she wore to Aunt Martha's wedding when we teenagers. I'm telling you that I saw her. And I'm not crazy.

ELEANOR. I don't think you're crazy. And I've never called you crazy. You just need to calm down. You know what Dr. Thune said about your heart. It can't take too much excitement. And here you go putting your life in danger.

FELISHA. I'm not seeking her out, Eleanor. She appears. It's the eleventh time!

ELEANOR. Just breathe. There has to be a logical explanation. Let me get you a glass of water.

FELISHA. I don't need any water. I'm perfectly fine. I'm just a little . . . flustered. (Pause.) I've missed her so, Eleanor.

ELEANOR. I know. I know.

FELISHA. And all these years, we've been here together, in this house. You've been so kind. And patient.

ELEANOR. You're my sister.

FELISHA. I know, but I've taken Mother's passing much harder than you. It must have been difficult.

ELEANOR. You're my sister.

FELISHA. And it's just the two of us. And this house. We didn't have to worry about lawyers or dividing anything up. We've been alright, right?

ELEANOR. You know we have. We didn't worry about all that silly legal mumbo-jumbo. We just took care of the house. And we've preserved the entire fortune.

FELISHA. Mother's fortune.

ELEANOR. Mother's fortune. And ours.

FELISHA. And ours. (*Pause.*) Eleanor, I don't understand why I keep seeing Mother. And she looks so strong, so tall, so youthful. It's almost like a revision of memory.

ELEANOR. I don't know, Felisha. Perhaps, your mind is playing tricks on you. You think about her all the time. Plus, all the heart medication may have some strange side effects. The doctor warned you about that.

FELISHA. I don't see how it's all possible.

ELEANOR. But when he gave you the medication, that was when you started seeing Mother, right?

FELISHA. (*Thinking. Then slowly.*) Right. But it's so real. Oh, I feel it in my chest now. I wonder if the medication is actually helping me. I sometimes think it's just candy or mints.

ELEANOR. They're expensive mints, then.

FELISHA. I need to go lie down. I'm starting to get dizzy.

ELEANOR. You do that. Have a lie down and get some rest.

As FELISHA starts to rise, another figure, with the appearance of a woman wearing a dress and a hat appears.

FELISHA. Eleanor!

ELEANOR. What?! What's wrong?

FELISHA. (*Points to woman*) Look!

ELEANOR. At what?

FELISHA. There! Don't you see her!?

ELEANOR. Where?

FELISHA. There! It's Mother.

ELEANOR. Oh, Felisha.

FELISHA. You don't see her? She's right there!

ELEANOR. Felisha, you need to go and get some rest.

FELISHA. No! She's right there. I can't believe you can't see her! She's just standing. It's Mother.

ELEANOR. You're very tired.

FELISHA. I'm not tired. And I'm not hallucinating! She's standing right there.

ELEANOR. (*Walking toward "Mother"*) Where? Here? Over here?

FELISHA. You're close! She's there.

ELEANOR. (*Near Mother*) No one is here, Felisha.

FELISHA.   I see her. Oh, she looks so strong and youthful.

ELEANOR.   (*Moving back to sit near where Felisha is standing*) I'm worried about you.

FELISHA.   My heart is fluttering a bit. I do need to sit. But she's there. And she's beautiful.

ELEANOR.   All right, Felisha. If she's really there, she can answer your questions. Ask her.

FELISHA.   What?

ELEANOR.   Ask her.

FELISHA.   What are you suggesting?

ELEANOR.   Ask her what you've been wanting to ask her all these years.

FELISHA.   I couldn't!

ELEANOR.   Why not? She's standing there. She hasn't left. If she's really there and you can see her, that means she's here for you, not me. So, ask her.

FELISHA.   If would be so disrespectful, so . . .

ELEANOR.   She's here for some reason.

FELISHA.   I haven't heard her voice.

ELEANOR.   Because you haven't asked her a question. You know what you want to know.

FELISHA.   (*Thinking*) Um, Mother. How are you? Um. Uh. I'm very glad you've come to see me. Eleanor says hello. She's having a hard time seeing you, but she's here, asking me to talk with you for us.

ELEANOR.   For you, Felisha. Ask.

FELISHA.   Mother. Uh. You've been gone from us quite a while. We're both older women now, but we managed to keep the house, and we've taken care of your . . . estate, your money that you got from Granddad. We haven't even divided it between us. We kept it as yours, as ours. And we . . . Pardon me. My heart isn't great, and it tends to beat too fast at times.

ELEANOR.   Ask her.

FELISHA.   Well, you left us. I know you didn't want to. And ever since then, since the doctors couldn't tell exactly what happened, it's been on my mind. Dr. Maddox made a statement that something someone said or did could have triggered your health and been the reason for your . . . passing. I have to know. I don't expect you to tell me exactly what happened, but I've wondered, really been obsessed with knowing who it was that caused you to slide into grief or pain or even . . . death. I know Aunt Tilly used to say harsh things. I know your brother Barton

26

was a disappointment to Granddad and Grandmother. Who, who hurt you so much that it took you from us? I have to know. I have to know.

Mother slowly lifts her hand and points to FELISHA.

FELISHA.   What? What? *(She holds her heart.)*

ELEANOR stands up and walks to FELISHA.

ELEANOR.   Are you okay?

FELISHA.   *(Crying, holding her chest)* No! No!

ELEANOR.   What is it?

FELISHA.   Not me! No, Mother.

Mother nods her head. Felisha holds her chest and begins to collapse.

ELEANOR.   Felisha! Felisha! Are you all right? Felisha!

FELISHA dies.

ELEANOR stands up, straightens her clothes, and walks over to Mother.

The actor playing Mother takes off his hat and wig and steps out of his dress.

ELEANOR.   So, "Mother," it took twelve times, twelve times for her to ask.

GRANT.   A lucky dozen.

ELEANOR goes up to Grant and holds him in a romantic embrace, looking his in the face.

ELEANOR.   Lucky is the word. Nothing to divide. No lawyers needed. Just you. Just me. Just Mother's "fortune." Just our fortune.

GRANT.   So, can I stick with my normal clothes now?

ELEANOR.   As long as you stick with me.

GRANT.   I'll get out of here so you can call the ambulance.

ELEANOR.   You do that. I'll call you later.

GRANT.   Okay. Remember: the grieving sister. You just watched your only living relative die. Tears. Sobs. You know the drill.

ELEANOR.   I know what I'm doing. You get out of here.

He leaves.

ELEANOR.   *(Dials phone)* Hello, something horrible has just happened! Just horrible!

Short Play 4/Scene 4—
Lucky Strike

HEIDI and ISABEL sit down at a diner table. Both ladies are visibly exhausted.

HEIDI.   If I don't get some coffee soon, I'll keel over from pure exhaustion.

ISABEL.   We've been driving nonstop for ten hours. It's understandable. We need caffeine. Well, you do more than I do. You've done the lion's share of driving.

HEIDI.   We've both done our share. Let's eat and find a place to sleep for a few hours.

JACKIE, a waitress approaches.

JACKIE.   Hello, darlings! How're y'all today?

HEIDI.   We're good.

ISABEL.   Fine.

JACKIE.   Could I get you beautiful girls something to drink? Maybe some coffee? Made fresh.

HEIDI.   That sounds perfect.

ISABEL.   We could really use . . .

JACKIE.   Two coffees, it is. Cream and sugar, all creamy and sweet.

HEIDI.   I actually don't like anything in my coffee. I like it hot and black.

JACKIE.   (*Chuckling*) That's ridiculous. Coffee needs a little flavor, a little something to cover up that bite.

HEIDI.   Okay. That being said, I'd still like it black. I can't drink it with anything in it.

ISABEL.   And I just want creamer. No sugar.

JACKIE.   It'll be okay. There's a process to becoming a coffee connoisseur.

ISABEL.   Please. Just creamer.

HEIDI.   Black. Black.

JACKIE.   Well, darling. I'll tell you something I'll do. I'll bring you the coffee "as is," and I'll bring all the good stuff on the side. You'll see what you can do, and you'll do the right thing.

HEIDI.   Just black, ma'am.

29

JACKIE.   (*smiling*, writing on her pad) You ladies are tough cookies. Reminds me of my mother. Whoa! Nelly!

ISABEL.   What is that supposed to mean?

JACKIE.   Compliments, ma'am. Compliments! I loved my momma. She was an angel sent from Heaven. Helped me through some of the most painful things anybody could go through. Life can be a living hell. It takes love to make it through it all.

HEIDI.   Do you have any specials today?

JACKIE.   The love of a momma. (*Back to reality*) Specials? Oh, yeah. We have a southwestern meatloaf with bell-pepper mashed taters and cream-style corn. We have Miss Madie's Southern Fried Chicken Legs with purple-hull peas and hot-water cornbread, and we have sauerkraut with Polish sausage served with pan-fried potatoes and Cajun-boiled corn on the cob. And we're talking corn doused in real cow butter.

ISABEL.   (*condescending and incredulous*) Cow butter.

JACKIE.   Cow. Butter. From a cow. Butter. The real deal. Where you two young ladies from?

HEIDI.   Tampa. Can we see a menu?

JACKIE.   You're a long way from home. You don't want one of the specials?

HEIDI.   Yeah. We're on a road trip of sorts. Not really. I'm really not hungry for any of those.

JACKIE.   Road trips. I did that once when I was younger. You've driven a long way. My brother went to Tampa once. Never told me why. Come on, all three of those are dee-licious to the bone. Well, only the chicken legs officially have bones, but you smell what I'm cooking here.

ISABEL.   What?

JACKIE.   You know. You see the handwriting on the Winnebago, you hear the vinyl on the record scratch, you feel the biceps on the hot guy, you taste the fumes of the gasoline that you accidently poured out as you were filling up your mower, you smell that coffee.

ISABEL.   Not yet. Still waiting on the coffee. And . . . what?

HEIDI.   We've been on the road for a long time and just need some food.

JACKIE.   Perfectly understandable. And food you'll get. Welcome to East Texas. Stay here on the Piney Woods side. The left side of East Texas is too much like . . . (*whispering*) Austin.

HEIDI.   Thanks for the advice. But we're actually heading to . . .

ISABEL.   Can we please get our coffee before we dehydrate into dust?

JACKIE.   Darling, I ain't no doctor, but I can tell you that there ain't no way you can
            dehydrate into dust. You're just using . . .

ISABEL.   Hyperbole.

JACKIE.   No, darling. There ain't no purple in my uniform. I hate purple, wouldn't work
            here if Jeffy had it in the get up.

HEIDI.   What?

ISABEL.   Can we please get our coffee? Please?

JACKIE.   Patience is a virtue.

ISABEL.   You have no idea how much I'm exercising it.

JACKIE.   Oh, I can tell. You look like you hit the gym a lot. Must go six, seven days a
            week. Darling, I can tell that you're not naturally thin. You're thick, like . . .
            thick. Tree trunk. Bear leg. Hind quarters thick. But you look good. You work
            hard not to look bad. I admire that. I'll get your coffee. I'll bet you're famished.

JACKIE leaves. HEIDI and ISABEL look at each other in shock for a few seconds.

HEIDI.   What was that?

ISABEL.   Did she just call me fat?

HEIDI.   I think she just complimented you on overcoming your natural disposition toward
            being fat.

ISABEL.   And I don't think she's doing it on purpose.

HEIDI.   Why did we do this again? This was a mistake.

ISABEL.   Stop it. It was no mistake. Heidi, this is for you. We're doing this to put a rest to
            all your . . . unrest. We're stopping here for a bit of something to eat and heading
            on up to Tulsa to see what we can find out.

HEIDI.   But why? I've lived my whole life perfectly okay. I have my job. I have Devin.
            I have a family who loves me. I have you and Corey for friends. Why do I have
            to come all the up here to dig up the past?

ISABEL.   Because you have a past just a few hours up the road.

HEIDI.   And why did I drag you all the way across the country?

ISABEL. You didn't drag me. I volunteered. In fact, I insisted that you do this. There is a chapter in your life that you have to dig into. It's eaten you alive for as long as I've known you. I'm with you to put it to rest.

HEIDI. You're the best friend a girl would ever ask for.

ISABEL. And once we get past the roaring dragon here and get something to eat, we can get on our way.

HEIDI. Okay. It's been on my mind for years, and I never would have known where to look if that strange man hadn't shown up right when I graduated high school and told me about Tulsa. I don't know whether to be happy that he came or to hate him for coming.

ISABEL. It is what it is. You can't un-hear it. At least we can go and see for ourselves.

HEIDI. Rosemary Branch Avenue in Tulsa. Rosemary Branch Avenue.

ISABEL. And we're going to see it for ourselves.

HEIDI. I don't know if I can. The scene of the crime and all.

ISABEL. You're grown. You were a little, little girl. You just need closure.

JACKIE enters.

JACKIE. And here's your coffee. And here's all the good stuff to make it drinkable. Please doctor it up. I just hate to see people drink poison.

HEIDI. Thank you.

ISABEL. We'll take care if it. Do you have a menu?

JACKIE. In the back room, but you don't need one.

ISABEL. Why's that?

JACKIE. You heard our specials. I don't know if you're trying to watch your figure and all, but those specials are near-bout the best food west of the Mississippi.

ISABEL. Notwithstanding, we'd really like to see some menus.

JACKIE. I'll have to go see if I can find some. Nobody ever uses them. The specials are like the sentinel for the town. Nobody in their right mind even thinks about ordering anything else.

ISABEL. I guess I'm suffering from mental disease because I'd actually like something else.

HEIDI. We're trying to stay away from fatty foods.

JACKIE. I can understand *her* (*indicating Isabel*) . . . but why are *you*?

32

HEIDI.	Health. Heart health. Cholesterol.
JACKIE.	You believe all that? Those TV doctors love to blow steam. Selling their mumbo jumbo.
ISABEL.	I'm actually a nurse. And I can tell you that . . .
JACKIE.	That eating fried chicken is bad for you?
ISABEL.	As a matter of fact . . .
JACKIE.	My grandma ate fried food every day, drank a quart of whisky every day, and smoked three cigars every day. She outlived four husbands and died at the age of 106. You can't tell me anything about eating. It's all bull.
HEIDI.	Do you have club sandwiches?
JACKIE.	We're not in a club, darling. This is just a regular restaurant. With tasty specials.
HEIDI.	Perhaps ham and cheese? As great at the specials sound, I'm just not all that hungry.
JACKIE.	Well, ham and cheese we can do. (*to Isabel*) Unless you think that pork is bad for you? Ham is pork, you know.
ISABEL.	Is it?
JACKIE.	It is, darling. And you'll eat it, and it won't hurt you. And you can eat and eat and drink whatever and smoke, and you'll be okay.
ISABEL.	Please don't talk smoking with me.
JACKIE.	Oh, it ain't cigarettes. I gave those up . . . a while back. Cigars, I'm telling you. Kept Granny alive. Kept her alive. That and pork fat. Just slicked up her for life, and kept sliding right through it.
HEIDI.	Can we get two ham and cheese sandwiches? We're going to have to head on up the road pretty soon.
JACKIE.	I'll go see what I can do. You two stay right here.
HEIDI.	We're planning on it.

JACKIE leaves.

ISABEL.	This coffee is like axel grease. It's stronger than mouthwash.
HEIDI.	Let's just eat and go.
ISABEL.	We still have a few hours to Tulsa. We need to rest while we can.
HEIDI.	This is such a weird place. Fitting for a weird trip. I don't need to know. I don't need to know anymore. I know enough.

ISABEL.   We've all told you that, but you know you want to know more. All of us have told you that the past is the past, but you can't move on totally. I mean you can't even set a wedding date with poor Devin.

HEIDI.   (*sarcastically*) Poor Devin.

ISABEL.   Yes, poor Devin. You know he adores you and has patiently waited for you to resolve all this.

HEIDI.   I know. I know.

ISABEL.   The best way is to just do it. No secrets. No hesitation. No tiptoeing around. Find out. Deal with it. Move on with life.

HEIDI.   You're right. You're totally right. No whining or being scared to whisper the truth. I have to find out exactly why everything happened the way it did. Why was she smoking? Why did she let the fire get out of control? Why didn't she try to save me? Why did it take her brother to run into that house on Rosemary Branch Avenue and drag a little girl to safety? No wonder I was taken. It was for the best. I know that. I just need to know why. And why did I end up in Tampa. I love my folks and all, but why?

ISABEL.   We can't find out everything, but we're going to drive up to Tulsa to find out enough for you to put this to rest. Maybe everything he told you was true. Maybe none of it was. But let's find out.

HEIDI.   Maybe she was drunk? Maybe she was selfish? He said she was just smoking away. Smoking. Lucky Strike cigarettes. That's what he said.

JACKIE appears.

JACKIE.   And here we are: two ham and cheese sandwiches for the traveling squad.

HEIDI.   Thank you.

JACKIE.   No problem.

ISABEL.   And what's this?

JACKIE.   Oh, that's some of our grilled potatoes. I know you just mentioned sandwiches, but I threw the side in, what do you call it . . . gratis?

ISABEL.   Thank you, but I'm not really looking for the extra carbs.

JACKIE.   Give 'em a try before you throw the baby out with the bathwater. They're really good. Jeffy actually grills 'em with onions and rosemary.

ISABEL and HEIDI look at each other with one-quarter grins.

HEIDI.   Good ol' rosemary.

ISABEL.	Can't get away from it, can we?
JACKIE.	I can take the potatoes back.
HEIDI.	No, it was the rosemary. Long story.
JACKIE.	Oh, tell me about it. It happens to me all the time. When Jeffy first started making these, I had the cringe factor for a few weeks. I used to live on a street called Rosemary, and it brought up bad memories.

ISABEL and HEIDI look at each other again.

JACKIE.	There you two go again with your private jokes. You're making me paranoid.
HEIDI.	(*to Jackie)* You lived on a street called Rosemary?
ISABEL.	(*to Heidi)* There have to be Rosemary streets all over the country.
JACKIE.	Yeah, I've seen a quite a few through the years. But yeah, it's been a while now, but I lived on Rosemary.
HEIDI.	A while?
JACKIE.	Yeah, several years. Why?
ISABEL.	It's nothing. (*to Heidi)* Think about where you are, Heidi. We're a solid six hours away.
JACKIE.	Of course, it wasn't around here.
ISABEL.	(*losing the momentum*) Of course.
JACKIE.	I don't like to think about it, but it wasn't just "Rosemary" anyway. It was Rosemary Branch Avenue up in Tulsa.

HEIDI puts her head on the table. Isabel stares at Jackie.

ISABEL.	Totally circumstantial!
JACKIE.	It wasn't a good time. That was the last place I lived before I left Tulsa. Bad situation. Painful. That's life, though, isn't it?
ISABEL.	Heidi, we need to go.
JACKIE.	You haven't even eaten.
HEIDI.	Oh, wow. Oh, wow.
JACKIE.	Are you all right, darling? You need to eat a lil' something. I don't have anything other than iced tea and cokes, but I do have a cigar if you need one. (*Giggles*)
ISABEL.	(*stopping and smiling*) Cigar?

JACKIE.   Yeah, a cigar. Maybe I shouldn't offer a cigar to a customer, but she looks like she needs a smoke.

ISABEL.   You're a cigar smoker?

JACKIE.   Yeah. Look, don't go judging me again. It's my life.

ISABEL.   No judgment. I promise. You smoke cigars?

JACKIE.   Yeah.

ISABEL.   Not cigarettes.

JACKIE.   No, not cigarettes.

ISABEL.   *(to Heidi)* See. Coincidence.

JACKIE.   Not anymore.

HEIDI.   What?

JACKIE.   Bad memories, darling. I had a . . . bad thing happen several years ago, and I gave up cigarettes. I did follow Granny's lead and pick up the cigars.

ISABEL.   You gave up the cigarettes?

JACKIE.   I did. I smoked 'em for years. Just one brand, though. Faithful to the brand. Until I couldn't be.

ISABEL.   Oh.

HEIDI.   The brand? The brand? Isabel?

JACKIE.   But I gave it up. Had to.

HEIDI.   The label?

ISABEL.   Heidi. Let's go.

HEIDI.   The brand. The brand.

JACKIE.   I had to give it up. It brought some bad, bad luck.

HEIDI.   The brand. What was the brand?

ISABEL.   No.

JACKIE.   Why?

HEIDI.   The brand?

ISABEL.   No.

JACKIE and HEIDI. Lucky Strike.

ISABEL and HEIDI stop and stare at each other.

JACKIE.   What?

ISABEL.   Let's go.

JACKIE.   You haven't eaten.

ISABEL.   (*Putting money on the table*) Here. This should cover all of it.

JACKIE.   Well, okay.

HEIDI.   *(as they are leaving)* I have to get out of here.

JACKIE.   Happy Trails. Oh, I never asked where you ladies are headed?

ISABEL and HEIDI look at each other.

ISABEL and HEIDI. Tampa.

JACKIE.   Wait. I thought that's where you came from?

ISABEL.   Exactly.

HEIDI.   (*looks at Jackie for a long time*) Good bye.

JACKIE.   Good bye, darlings.

HEIDI hesitates and then hugs a surprised JACKIE.

JACKIE.   Well, okay.

HEIDI.   Bye. (*walks out*)

ISABEL.   So, yeah. (*walks out*)

JACKIE.   Good bye. (*stands in shock a bit and then starts cleaning up*)

Short Play 5/Scene 5–
Luck of the Ire

KEENAN, a boy is crying, sitting on the side of his bed. His dad, LARRY, comes in.

LARRY.   Hey, buddy. You doing better?

KEENAN.   I guess.

LARRY.   You don't sound better.

KEENAN.   I'll be okay.

LARRY.   I know. You'll be fine. I just want to make sure you're breathing, blood still flowing (*he tussles Kennan's hair*), heart still beating.

KENNAN.   I'm okay, Dad.

LARRY.   We're going to fix all this. Don't you worry.

KENNAN.   It can't be fixed, Dad. It's just the way things happen.

LARRY.   No.

KENNAN.   Yes. I'm not as big at the other guys. They don't like me. They make fun of me all the time. Every day. I hate it. But it's not gonna change. Nobody changes. It's just what happens. There's nothing I can do.

LARRY.   But there's something I can do.

KENNAN.   Dad, there's nothing. You came to the school. It made things worse. Now even the teachers are mad at me. I just have to deal with it. I can be tough.

LARRY.   No. It's not gonna happen that way. No son of mine is going to be bullied.

KENNAN.   Already happened.

LARRY.   There's a solution.

KENNAN.   There's not.

LARRY.   Ready? (*standing*)

KENNAN.   What?

LARRY.   (Grinning) Ready?

KENNAN.   For what?

LARRY.   The solution. (*leaves the room and returns with a short man, tied up and gagged*)

For the duration of this scene, the "bound" man struggles and tries to talk.

KENNAN. Dad?

LARRY. Kennan, my boy. Look! Our problems are solved.

KENNAN. I don't understand. Who is this man? Why is he tied up?

LARRY. Kennan, look! Use your brain, my boy. Look. What do you see?

KENNAN. A crime?

LARRY. No! Look at him. It's a leprechaun!

KENNAN. A leprechaun?

LARRY. A leprechaun. Look at his body type. Look at his face and his arms and legs. He's the elusive little Irish wonder!

KENNAN. Wow! But why is he tied up?

LARRY. Because he has to be. I captured him. That's the only way that you can harness their power. They're sneaky little creatures, but if you capture one, you can make him do your bidding. It's like a genie. He has to grant you the wishes you wish.

KENNAN. Wow!

LARRY. Right! And we have one, son!

KENNAN. Wow!

LARRY. And you know what that means?

KENNAN. What?

LARRY. We're getting rid of your bullies.

KENNAN. Really?

LARRY. He's a leprechaun! They're hard to find, but if you can capture one, he's required to grant your wishes.

KENNAN. Is that the way it works? I didn't know that!

LARRY. Yes! It's old folklore, but it's true stuff.

KENNON. We read a story about them in school, but I never knew they were real.

LARRY. I'd forgotten their power until I saw one in one of the new video games I bought with Grandma's birthday money last week. Then I thought today, "That's it! We're going to get rid of Kennan's bullies once and for all!"

KENNON. Can he make them disappear?

LARRY.   Forever.

KENNON.   How?

LARRY.   Son, he's a leprechaun. He's magic. Those are the ways of the world.

KENNON.   I don't want them to die—or be hurt. I just want them to stop.

LARRY.   Or go away.

KENNON.   Maybe.

LARRY.   Let's see what we can do? (*He pulls the gag off of the bound man.*)

MILO.   Argh!

LARRY.   They're wily ones!

MILO.   Are you kidding me? A leprechaun? Let me go.

LARRY.   That's what they always say. Listen to him go on.

MILO.   Untie me. You're out of your mind.

LARRY.   Careful there, boy-o.

KENNON.   Boy-o?

LARRY.   I'm using the Irish lingo.

MILO.   What? Untie me! NOW!

LARRY.   Careful, wee one.

MILO.   Stop! Stop your ridiculous . . . words.

LARRY.   Temper, temper, little man.

MILO.   (*Calmly*) Listen to me carefully. I don't know whether you're pulling some kind of prank or if you're serious. In either case, you're breaking the law. I demand that you free me. Things will go a lot better for you if you do the right thing.

LARRY.   Listen to him go on and on, Kennan. They're sly creatures.

MILO.   My name is Milo. I'm English-Italian. I don't have a drop of Irish blood in me. And I'm not a LEPRECHAUN. There aren't any leprechauns!

LARRY.   The greatest trick of the devil is to convince men that he doesn't exist, eh? Eh, ye cute little leprechaun?

MILO.   (*gently, to Kennan*) Kennan, is that your name?

KENNAN.   He does speak English.

LARRY.   The Irish speak English, boy.

MILO.   I'm not Irish. I'm . . . okay.

LARRY.   And leprechauns speak all languages.

MILO.   They do not.

LARRY.   See, he IS a leprechaun!

MILO.   No! I'm just saying that leprechauns . . . No. There are no leprechauns. But if there were, they wouldn't speak all languages. Let me go. You are in so much trouble. This is kidnapping.

KENNAN.   Dad, can he hurt us?

LARRY.   Of course not. We're his masters. He has to do what we say. He has to use his magic to do what we want.

MILO.   I don't have magic. I'm a man. I'm a landscaper. I take care of yards. Mow. Weed. Flowers. All that stuff. I own my own business. I have seven employees. They'll know I'm missing.

LARRY.   See, son. He's spinning his tale, like Rumpelstiltskin. He sort of looks like Rumpelstiltskin.

KENNAN.   He does.

MILO.   STOP! Let me go. You're both insane. I'm not a leprechaun. There are NO leprechauns. They're fictional creatures. They have not, do not, and will not exist. Are you daft? You're living in a world of games and mythology. You've kidnapped a human being, and you'll go to jail!

LARRY.   I know that you things are ornery, but I'm getting tired of your mouth.

MILO.   You're getting tired? I'm the one tied up, brought who knows where, being held hostage!

LARRY.   It's time you settled down and act a bit more appreciative.

MILO.   (*incredulous*) What?

KENNAN.   Dad, what now?

LARRY.   What you do mean, my boy?

KENNAN.   What now? If it won't do what we ask, how are we going to get it to get rid of my bullies?

LARRY.   Oh, it'll do what we say. It has to. We own it.

KENNAN.   It says its name is Milo.

LARRY.   It's not Milo. It's a trick.

MILO.	My name is Milo.
LARRY.	It's not Milo. Milo is a human's name. Not a Leprechaun. It's probably something like Micranumbach or Hobblestone O'Blarney-Bottom or Liam O'Neeson O'Van Morrison-shire.
MILO.	I can't believe this.
KENNAN.	And he's going to take care of my bullies! Thank you, Hobblestone.
LARRY.	Ah, you also got the vibe that that was his name.
MILO.	What?
LARRY.	So, I was right. It was just an instinct, but I was right again. Hobblestone. Hobblestone O'Blarney-Bottom. You've got a special kind of magic, ain't you?
MILO.	You're serious? You actually believe what you're saying?
LARRY.	There's a whole lot more to this world than what we're told. Ah, the TV and the schools all try to tell us that everything is cut and dried, that "it" just "is what it is," but the truth lies in our games. In the stories. The truth is in the play world. There's a world where we eat little pellets and are chased by ghosts, there's a world in which I have a brother named Luigi, there's a world where I shoot zombies and slay vampires and live as an assassin in World War II. It's where I live. It's actually where we all live. That's all the real world. That's the truth, the messages the designers are sharing. And the world bleeds into the one I have to pay bills in. The realm of the real often loses villains that land in school houses and torture my son. They escape and punish me by hurting *him*, all because I know the truth. They're going to stop hurting him. They are going to stop. And you're going to stop them.
MILO.	*(in shock)* How? How can I stop them?
KENNAN.	You're Hobblestone. You can do anything.
LARRY.	Yeah, what he said.
MILO.	Are these *children* you're talking about?

NOVA, Larry's daughter, enters with her large boyfriend, OTIS.

NOVA.	What's going on here?
LARRY.	Nova.
KENNAN.	Nova! Look, Dad's caught a leprechaun named Hobblestone. He's going to get rid of my bullies.
NOVA.	What?

LARRY. It's true, sweetheart. I've been thinking and thinking about what to do about Kennan's trouble, and when I saw Hobblestone here, it just came to me!

NOVA. Are you serious, Dad?

LARRY. Of course, I'm serious. Look at him. He's a feisty little thing.

MILO. Nova? Is that your name? You have to listen to me . . .

NOVA. Are you really a leprechaun?

MILO. What? Of course not.

LARRY Of course he his.

KENNAN. He sure is!

NOVA. Dad. This is ridiculous.

MILO. Finally.

NOVA. What were you thinking?

MILO. Okay. Please. (*holding up his bound hands*)

NOVA. After all I've been through and you never tried to help me, and then you go and get Kennan his own leprechaun!

MILO. What? No!

NOVA. (*to Milo*) Shut up.

LARRY. Sweetheart, I've never seen one until today. I promise that if I'd seen one when you were younger, I would have grabbed him and made him help you.

NOVA. Really?

LARRY. Absolutely. I love you and Kennan both. If there's anything I can do to make your life better, I will.

MILO. I don't believe this.

LARRY. (*looking at OTIS*) Who's this?

NOVA. That's my new boyfriend, Otis.

Otis shakes hands with Larry and Kennan.

LARRY. Good to meet you, Otis.

OTIS. Hello.

KENNAN. Welcome to the family, Otis.

MILO. (*rolling his eyes*) Yeah, welcome to the family.

OTIS.   (*putting his hand on Milo's shoulder*) Hello, Hobblestone.

MILO.   It's Milo.

KENNAN.   It's Hobblestone.

MILO.   It's Milo.

LARRY.   It's Hobblestone O'Blarney-Bottom.

OTIS.   That's a funny name.

MILO.   It's not my name.

LARRY.   Yes, it is. Quiet! Or I'll lock you in the closet. But wait, you people like the dark.

MILO.   You people? What's that supposed to mean?

KENNAN.   He's not a people, Dad. He's a creature.

LARRY.   Right-o, son. Right-o.

OTIS.   It's nice to meet you, little . . . guy.

MILO.   The pleasure's all yours.

LARRY.   (*to Nova*) How long you been dating this guy?

NOVA.   Few weeks.

LARRY.   You've never mentioned him.

NOVA.   My business, Dad. I gotta have some privacy.

OTIS.   I'm a respectable man, Nova's dad.

LARRY.   The name's Larry. Larry Beauchamp.

MILO.   Good to know.

NOVA.   (*to Milo*) You have no legal rights. You're a mythical creature.

KENNAN.   When is it going to make my bullies go away?

LARRY.   Soon. (*to Milo*) So, Hobblestone. It's time. I captured you. I own you.

MILO.   (*to Nova and Otis*) Are you hearing this?

LARRY.   And you have to grant my wishes. It's canon. It's the law of the leprechauns. When you're not finding pots of gold, you're hiding from humans—because once we get you, you have to serve us. So, here we are. I am officially claiming ownership and demanding you get rid of Kennan's bullies. We won't ask any questions about what you actually do, but now is the time to do it. So, go. Do it.

MILO.   I can't do anything. I'm a man. I'm a hostage in your house.

LARRY.   This is going to get ugly. You CANNOT refuse me! I own you!

MILO.   You've kidnapped me! But you don't own me.

OTIS.   Let me handle it.

LARRY.   What?

OTIS.   All the rest of you step out, and let me handle this.

LARRY.   I know you're trying to help, Otis, but this is no concern of yours.

OTIS.   I think it is. And no matter, I need you to step out. I'll take care of . . . Hobblestone.

KENNAN.   Dad, maybe he'll get him to start granting the wish!

NOVA.   Give him a shot, Dad.

LARRY.   (*stares at Otis for a few seconds*) You think you can break him?

OTIS.   When you return to this room, I promise you that everything will be different.

LARRY.   You make this leprechaun do what I want, and you and I will be friends. *(offers Otis a handshake; Otis shakes his hand.)*

OTIS.   You'll be shocked.

LARRY.   Okay. Let's do it. Come on, Kennan, Nova. Some things are left unseen.

KENNAN.   Thank you, Otis.

NOVA.   Come on, kid.

LARRY.   (*as he is exiting*) I'm counting on you.

The room now holds just Otis and Milo.

OTIS.   So, here we are.

MILO.   I don't know what you have in mind, but I promise you that if you try to harm me, I'll do everything I can to hurt you.

OTIS.   You're talking pretty big, Hobblestone.

MILO.   You actually believe that I'm a leprechaun?

OTIS.   Are you?

MILO.   Of course not! Your new best friend is insane.

OTIS.   (*Moving toward Milo*) And who would that be?

MILO.   Your girlfriend's dad.

OTIS.   She's not my girlfriend.

He starts to untie Milo.

MILO.   What?

OTIS.   She's not my girlfriend. And you're not a leprechaun.

MILO.   What?

OTIS.   Are you?

MILO.   No. No!

OTIS.   And the one last month wasn't a vampire, and the one a week before that wasn't an elf.

MILO.   Are you kidding me? Who are you?

OTIS.   Officer John Brody, Police and Rescue.

MILO.   Thank God!

Milo stands and stretches.

OTIS.   We need to get you out of here.

MILO.   (*the impact of the revelation hitting him afresh*) Others? Other people have been kidnapped, and you haven't arrested these people?

OTIS.   We didn't know it until earlier today. They'd been held and then threatened when released. The daughter came to us today to give us a heads up. I'm here. She figured someone else was in the loop.

MILO.   What about the kid, his bullies?

OTIS.   All a ruse. Kid's got problems. Dad's easily manipulated. The kid's been bullying others. The dad's been called about it dozens of times. All that doesn't matter. We have to get you out of here.

MILO.   He sounded so believable. They both did.

OTIS.   Sir, we have to get you out of here.

MILO.   Does the dad believe all of this? That I'm a leprechaun? He doesn't realize his kid's a bully?

OTIS.   Sir, I don't know. Let's go!

MILO.   KENNAN!

OTIS.   What are you doing?

MILO.   (*In an Irish accent*) KENNAN! Get yourself in here!

OTIS.   Sir, you have to go. We have an arrest to make.

KENNAN.   (*entering, smiling*) What? You're helping me?

MILO.   In more ways than you'll ever know.

KENNAN.   I knew it. I knew you're a leprechaun. You're going to destroy my enemies!

NOVA.   (*entering*) What's happening? Otis?

OTIS.   Sir!

LARRY.   (*entering*) Is he still fighting you?

OTIS.   (*to Nova*) Get him (*indicating Milo*) out of here.

LARRY.   What?

KENNAN.   Dad! He's going to get rid of the bullies.

LARRY.   He's what?

MILO.   (*Nova grabbing him. He speaks dramatically and with an Irish dialect*) Kennan, my boy. I know the truth! I know what *you've* done!

LARRY.   Shut up!

OTIS.   Nova, get him out of here.

MILO.   I know that *you're* the bully! I know that you've abused *others*! Know this: a curse now lies on you and your family.

NOVA.   Stop.

OTIS.   You're making things worse.

LARRY.   Don't confuse my boy. Don't listen to him, Kennan.

KENNAN.   Dad! He's a leprechaun. What is he saying?

MILO.   You're the bully. But no longer! A curse on you! Just wait 'til you see! A curse.

NOVA.   Come on. (*drags Milo offstage*)

MILO.   A curse!!

KENNAN.   What? What have I done?

LARRY.   He's a liar, Kennan.

KENNAN.   I'm the bully?

LARRY.   No.

OTIS.   (*pulling out handcuffs and placing them on Larry*) Sir, you're under arrest . . .

LARRY.   What?

OTIS.   . . . for abduction, kidnapping, and holding hostage . . .

LARRY.   Wait.

KENNAN.   What?

LARRY.   You're a cop?

OTIS.   Come with me, sir. You have the right to remain silent.

KENNAN.   Dad.

Otis leads Larry out. Kennan follows, confused.

OTIS.   Anything you say can and will be used against you in a court of law. You have
            the right to an attorney . . .

Short Play 6/Scene 6—
Luck and War

PETER, a man in a tuxedo, sits down, upset, despondent, depressed. He breathes heavily, puts
his head in his hands. His brother, Quin, sits down beside him. They sit quietly
for several seconds.

QUIN. (*Searching for the right words*) You okay? (*no response*) Hey, are you breathing
there?

PETER. I'm okay.

QUIN. That's not really a fair question to ask.

PETER. It's fine. It's hard to come up with something to say.

QUIN. Yeah.

PETER. Wow. I didn't see this coming. (*Laughs bitterly*) Why didn't I see this one
coming, Quin? I missed all the signs.

QUIN. There's no way you could have known.

PETER. I should have, though. There had to have been some signs. Months, Quin.
Months. Planning. Invitations. (*Laughs*) Cakes. The honeymoon's paid for! In
full! And think of the people who flew out here. Man!

QUIN. If it helps, we can use the honeymoon as a vacation. And Aunt Lorraine enjoyed
getting out of Alaska.

PETER. I'm sure Alaska was glad she left for a few days, too.

They both laugh.

QUIN. And we can give the cakes to the homeless.

PETER. Promoting nutrition in the less fortunate.

QUIN. You're going to be okay, Peter. You're strong.

PETER. I don't feel strong.

QUIN. But you are. I mean . . . you . . . handled it . . . all . . . so much better than I would
have.

PETER. It wasn't choice. I was in shock. I mean. There I was: standing there. You were
right there. Everyone was. And it was . . . a nightmare.

QUIN. You don't have to . . .

PETER. Please. Let me.

QUIN. Okay.

PETER. I mean . . . "The Wedding March." Mendelsohn echoing through the church. And there she was. I smiled at her. I smiled at her, Quin. I thought it was about to happen THE WAY WE REHEARSED! The WAY we PLANNED!

QUIN. I know.

PETER. And she, she, she, waved her lacey arm to stop it all. The music. Everything. A wave, and she ends everything. And then she said, she said . . .

QUIN. I know. You don't have to . . .

PETER. "I can't do this. I don't love you, Peter. Good luck with your life."

QUIN. Cold.

PETER. Good luck with your life!

QUIN. And you were so mannerly, Peter. You didn't scream. You didn't curse. You just . . .

PETER. I let her walk away and make a fool out of me. Everybody I know is laughing at me right now.

QUIN. No! Not at all, brother. No one is laughing at you. They are all angry at her! You should have heard some of the things Uncle Ed and Morty and Jennifer were saying. They want to give her a piece of their mind.

PETER. Wouldn't do any good.

QUIN. If Mom were still alive, she would have followed her out of this church and ripped her head off. I can just hear her: "How dare you do that to my son." She would have tracked her down and made her life miserable.

PETER. That may be why Mom's not around anymore.

QUIN. (Smiling, hitting Peter on the knee.) Stop! That was our mother.

PETER. She could be spiteful.

QUIN. True.

PETER. Whew! (Standing up.) What now? Can I show my face? We still have a few dozen people in the reception hall, right?

QUIN. Yeah, a few.

PETER. Well, I don't want to see them. And why are there still so many cars outside? Where did everybody else go?

QUIN. Those are from the church next door. There's, uh, another wedding taking place over there.

PETER. (*Hands up with frustration*) Great. Just great. I wish them both the greatest of happiness.

QUIN. You know they're not . . .

PETER. I know. I know. Ugh!

RACHEL, in a wedding dress, runs in, follows by SAVANNAH, in a bridesmaid dress.

RACHEL. Oh, great. Someone's in here, too!

SAVANNAH. Rachel, stop running.

QUIN. Everything okay?

RACHEL. Does it look okay? *(to Savannah)* Does everything LOOK okay?

SAVANNAH. Sorry to interrupt. We've got a problem here.

PETER. Tell me about it.

RACHEL. Don't even talk to me about problems.

SAVANNAH. Rachel.

RACHEL. You didn't have your WHOLE world fall apart today.

PETER. As a matter of fact . . .

RACHEL. Nothing could have happened to YOU that would compare to what JUST happened to me.

QUIN. Actually, if you could just try to . . .

SAVANNAH. She just had a horrible thing . . .

QUIN. HE just had a horrible thing . . .

PETER and RACHEL. I'm right here.

SAVANNAH and QUIN. (*to each other*) He/she was just left at the altar.

SAVANNAH and QUIN. (*straight ahead*) Oh. (*looking back at each other, realizing the irony*) Oooh.

RACHEL. Wait. You were just jilted?

PETER. I guess you can put it that way.

RACHEL.   That's what it is.

PETER.   Well, you were jilted, too, then.

RACHEL.   Going for the kill. Yes. Jilted. Left. He didn't show up.

QUIN.   *(to Savannah)* That's rough. Peter's showed up and made a scene. In front of everyone.

SAVANNAH. That's just terrible.

QUIN.   Yeah, it was. He's devastated. It's wrecked him.

SAVANNAH. Poor baby.

PETER.   *(to Rachel)* Am I here?

RACHEL.   Evidently YOU are. You've become the star of the show.

PETER.   It's not a show or a contest.

RACHEL.   Everything's a contest.

SAVANNAH. *(to Quin)* And she hates it if she's not the star.

RACHEL.   Am "I" here?

SAVANNAH. Yes, Rach. I'm sorry. I know today's been an embarrassment. People are going to be talking about this for years.

RACHEL.   *(Sits and cries)* Agh!

SAVANNAH. *(Comforting her)* Oh, Rachel. It'll be okay. It wasn't your fault. It was Marshall.

PETER.   *(sitting, then to Quin)* I can't believe any of this.

RACHEL.   *(to Savannah)* Don't mention his name.

QUIN.   *(sitting between Peter and Savannah)* I'm sorry.

SAVANNAH. *(to Rachel)* Sorry.

PETER.   *(to Quin)* What was she thinking?

RACHEL.   *(to Savannah)* He's going down in flames for this.

QUIN.   *(to Peter)* It was unheard of.

SAVANNAH. *(to Rachel)* It was uncalled for.

PETER.   *(to Quin)* People are going to think that "I" did something wrong.

RACHEL.   *(to Savannah)* He'll wish he'd never met me.

QUIN.   *(to Peter)* People know you. They know your reputation.

SAVANNAH. (*to Rachel*) We'll preserve your reputation.

PETER.   (*to Quin*) You're good to me.

RACHEL.   (*to Savannah*) My reputation? He's the one who'd besmirched his own identity.

QUIN.   (*to Peter*) True.

SAVANNAH. (*to Rachel*) True.

RACHEL.   (*looking straight ahead*) Men.

PETER.   (*looking straight ahead*) Women.

Rachel and Peter lean out and look over at each other. They smirk.

Quin and Savannah look at each other. Quin offers a handshake.

QUIN.   Name's Quin.

SAVANNAH. (*shaking his hand*) Savannah.

QUIN.   Nice to meet you, Savannah.

SAVANNAH. Likewise.

RACHEL.   (*standing*) Quit fraternizing with the enemy.

QUIN.   What?

PETER.   Leave him alone. He hasn't done anything to you.

RACHEL.   Don't be rude to me on my wedding day!

PETER.   Evidently, it's NOT your wedding day.

RACHEL.   Well, it's certainly not yours.

SAVANNAH. See what I have to deal with? (*indicating Rachel*)

QUIN.   I get it. Look at mine. (*indicating Peter*)

SAVANNAH. You the best man?

QUIN.   Yep. Maid of honor?

SAVANNAH. Figured. And yes.

QUIN.   Figured as well.

RACHEL.   Do you two need to get a room?

PETER.   (*to Rachel*) Why did you even come in here? This was my church.

RACHEL.   I, um. UGH! I was trying to get away. There were too many people next door. And your church is a lot smaller. In fact, you could only get a third of the people from my wedding in this room. You had a much smaller crowd than I did.

SAVANNAH. Here we go again. Rachel, please, you've both been though a lot today.

PETER.   My crowd may have been smaller, but that means that three times as many people saw YOU get humiliated. My number is smaller!

QUIN.   (*Pulls out his phone and looks at it*) Oh, no.

PETER.   What?

SAVANNAH. What?

QUIN.   Peter. Uh. Uh. Sandy Bolton recorded it all, everything Kimberly did and, uh, said and, uh . . .

PETER.   And what?

QUIN.   Posted it on YouTube. It's already been viewed over 2000 times.

RACHEL.   (*as if spiking a ball*) Ha! Multiply *THAT* three times as many.

PETER.   (*Sits down again, almost hyperventilating*) Oh! Oh! SANDY! I'm going to kill her.

RACHEL.   All's fair in love and war.

QUIN.   (*to Savannah*) Is she always like this?

SAVANNAH. (*to Quin*) Somebody's got to be her friend.

PETER.   (*to Rachel*) So, is this love or war?

QUIN.   (*to Savannah*) You're a patient woman.

SAVANNAH. (*to Quin*) So are you. Not a woman. I mean you're definitely not a woman.

RACHEL.   (*to Peter*) Is there a difference?

QUIN.   (*to Savannah*) I'm glad you can tell.

PETER.   (*to Rachel*) I guess not. Not after today.

SAVANNAH. (*to Quin*) I could tell from the beginning.

PETER.   (*to Quin*) Seriously? I mean, seriously! Now? This?

QUIN.   What?

PETER.   I'm not blind.

SAVANNAH. What?

RACHEL.   Or deaf!

SAVANNAH and QUIN.   (*look at each other*) Wow.

RACHEL.   How can you seriously have anything to do with that? (*points at Quin*)

SAVANNAH and PETER.   Wait a minute.

PETER.   Quin Marino is one of the most honorable men I've ever met in my life. And on top of that, he's my brother.

QUIN.   Thanks, bro.

SAVANNAH. (*to Quin*) Marino? Italian. Oooh. I like.

RACHEL.   Your brother? Oh, great. That figures.

SAVANNAH. (*to Quin*) We're MacGuires. Scottish. And yes, she's my sister.

QUIN.   Pleasure to meet you, Savannah MacGuire. (*Savannah giggles.*)

PETER.   What's happening?

RACHEL.   Your brother.

PETER.   Your sister.

RACHEL.   You were jilted.

PETER.   And YOU were jilted.

RACHEL.   You're on YouTube.

PETER.   (*looking around in anger*) Sandy!

SAVANNAH. Your brother (*searching for his name*) . . .

QUIN.   Peter.

SAVANNAH. Yeah, Peter.   Peter has a temper.

QUIN.   He does.

SAVANNAH. Is that an Italian thing?

QUIN.   It's a Peter thing. To be fair, it's been a bad day for him.

SAVANNAH. True.

RACHEL.   Savannah Michelle MacGuire, have you forgotten . . .

QUIN.   Michelle. That's pretty. It goes well with your name.

SAVANNAH. Thank you. And yours?

QUIN.   Eh. (*smiling*)

SAVANNAH. Come on . . . (leading him)

QUIN. (giving in) Quinton Antonio Marino.

SAVANNAH. Sexy!

RACHEL. I'm out of here. Savannah, just do whatever.

SAVANNAH. Nobody'll know you back in the reception at this wedding. (to Quin) Oh, are your people still back there? Can she go get some punch or something?

QUIN. Sure. No problem.

RACHEL. I don't believe this. I . . . you . . . I just . . . (giving up) Which way's the punch?

QUIN. Right through there (pointing)

Rachel storms out.

SAVANNAH. You're so sweet. (pauses) And cute.

PETER. (looking at them) How is this even possible? What's this? Five minutes? Do I need to call Guinness?

QUIN. (pulling out phone again) Oh, wow. Sandy's posted more. This is you sitting down by the altar after Kimberly left.

PETER. (Coming over to look) What?!

QUIN. And of Kimberly driving away and waving. How'd she get that? Wow. Hey, she's added a little selfie part. Oh, that's . . . Uh. (looking up at Peter)

PETER. What?

QUIN. She's, uh, back in the kitchen. This footage is back with the reception.

PETER. (storming out) I'm going to kill her. Sandy!!

SAVANNAH. Well, well. Here we are.

QUIN. Indeed. Here we are.

SAVANNAH. We both have some hotheads in our families.

QUIN. We do. (pause) And I'll bet we both keep the peace.

SAVANNAH. Always have. Calming force. Even with Mom and Dad.

QUIN. My mom's been gone for a while, but I definitely keep my dad in check. Along with Peter.

SAVANNAH. We're two of a kind.

QUIN. Two peas in a pod.

SAVANNAH. Just perfect for each . . . other.

QUIN. I think so, too.

SAVANNAH. You do?

QUIN. I do.

SAVANNAH. Okay.

QUIN. You know what I'm thinking?

SAVANNAH. I don't know. It may be what I'm thinking.

QUIN. If it is, I like it.

SAVANNAH. It probably is, and I like that you like it.

QUIN. You know what we have two of here?

SAVANNAH. Other than us?

QUIN. Yep.

SAVANNAH. I think I know.

QUIN. Two churches

SAVANNAH. Two ministers, well, yours may be a priest.

QUIN. He's a minister. Kimberly's Methodist.

SAVANNAH. Understandable. The church and all. The name on the door.

QUIN. A dead giveaway.

SAVANNAH. Right.

QUIN. Two receptions.

SAVANNAH. All our families. Even the YouTubers.

QUIN. So, do we?

SAVANNAH. You want to?

QUIN. Do you?

SAVANNAH. Are you asking?

QUIN. Do you want me to?

SAVANNAH. Only if you want to.

QUIN. I do.

SAVANNAH. I like the sound of that. Just ask.

QUIN.   I will.

SAVANNAH. Do it.

QUIN.   Savannah Michelle MacGuire, will you marry me?

SAVANNAH. I thought you'd never ask.

QUIN.   Is that a yes?

SAVANNAH. Of course, it's a yes.

QUIN.   Yes!

They kiss.

SAVANNAH. Wait, we have two ministers in two churches. Which one do we use?

QUIN.   Well, Peter and . . .

SAVANNAH. Rachel.

QUIN.   Yeah, Peter and Rachel are back there.

SAVANNAH and QUIN.   Next door then!

Quin picks Savannah up in his arms to carry her next door.

SAVANNAH. My family's going to love you.

QUIN.   I'm trying to decide whether or not to invite mine.

He carries her toward the exit.

SAVANNAH. Could they make such a long trip, fit it on their calendars?

QUIN.   I'll text Sandy when I get next door. Maybe she can film it and send them a copy.

SAVANNAH. I won the contest!

They exit.

Short Play 7/Scene 7—
As Luck Would Have It

During this course of this conversation, VINCENT is pacing on another part of stage, thinking.
He is in a locked "hospital cell" of some kind.

Detective TERRY Tolson and Dr. USHA Ullman watch VINCENT while they talk.

TERRY.   So, what does he think?

USHA.   Who actually knows?

TERRY.   Well, I would assume that *you* would.

USHA.   I'm not a mind reader.

TERRY.   You're the closest thing we have to it.

USHA.   It's not exactly open: his mind.   He closes it off to anything and anyone while he's thinking.

TERRY.   That much we already know. Plus, he's always thinking. (*pause*) Does he assume that he's going home, that all's well?

USHA.   That, I *can* answer. Yes. All indicators point to his assumption that he is visiting for a bit and going back to his home very soon.

TERRY.   He's too smart. He's too determined. He's too unpredictable, Doctor.

USHA.   I know, Detective. He has firmly planted his realty in his mind. And when a mind is as brilliant as his, as creative as his, the slightest distortion of reality can give him motivation to take matters into his own hands.

TERRY.   And that's precisely why he's here.

USHA.   He's here because you're scared of him and he's convinced that the police don't see the danger that he sees.

TERRY.   I'm not your patient, Doctor. And I'm not here for your assessment of the police force. I need to know if you can keep him here, keep him off the streets, out of our business so we can do our jobs. We don't need vigilante detectives hunting imaginary suspects based on fabricated realities. The city would go wild.

USHA.   Well, I can't lock him away and throw away the key. He has rights.

TERRY.   So do the people of this city, Dr. Ullman.

USHA.   And that's why he's here. Temporarily.

61

TERRY.   We can't have people going out and conducting investigations. It's dangerous. It's not normal.

USHA.   Normal is extremely relative. And is it illegal to investigate?

TERRY.   I should have known when I met you that you'd be one of *those* doctors.

USHA.   Ones who look out for patients?

TERRY.   And forget the general public? You care for the minority. I protect the majority.

USHA.   Are you finished, detective?

TERRY.   It depends. What are you going to do about Vincent?

USHA.   He's not a danger to himself. He's not a danger to others.

TERRY.   You're serious. (*turning and breathing heavily, frustrated*) May I see him?

USHA.   Planning on harassing him? Purposely irritating him?

TERRY.   No. (*pause*) Just planning on talking. With you there.

USHA.   (*Thinking*) Okay. But he's on his way out as of now, and until he is, he's a patient—of mine.

TERRY.   Let me talk to him.

USHA walks to the area where VINCENT walks, slides a card and enters the area. TERRY follows.

USHA.   Hello, Vincent.

Vincent does not respond; he remains focused on his own thinking.

TERRY.   So, Vincent. Convincing Dr. Ullman that you're harmless I see.

USHA.   Detective, you promised.

TERRY.   I promised you nothing, Doctor.

VINCENT.   Detective Tolson is careful with words, Doctor. I'm sure no promises were made.

USHA.   I won't allow games being played, not on my watch.

VINCENT.   It's okay, Doctor. The detective doesn't play games. Never has.

USHA.   Nonetheless, Vincent, I have to tell you that I have found no reason to keep you against your will. If you're . . .

TERRY.   Wait, Doctor. Before you say anything else, I need you to think about a few things.

USHA.   Detective. No games.

TERRY.   Humor me. For a moment.

VINCENT.   Patience, Doctor. It makes you virtuous.

USHA.   Go ahead.

TERRY.   Vincent, what are you up to?

VINCENT.   You know exactly what I'm doing. You know my goals.

TERRY.   And you know my concerns.

VINCENT.   And you know that I'm not a threat to you.

TERRY.   Not personally, but you are a threat to my investigation.

VINCENT.   I'm actually helping you.

TERRY.   I don't need your help.

VINCENT.   Yes, you do. Immensely.

TERRY.   There you go again.

VINCENT.   I go again because I'm integral to your success in this case.

TERRY.   You're not a part of the police.

VINCENT.   So, you lock me up in here.

TERRY.   You're not locked up.

VINCENT.   And yet, here I am.

TERRY.   Not locked up.

VINCENT.   And yet, you stop Dr. Ullman when she is about to release me.

TERRY.   To talk with you

VINCENT.   Against my will

TERRY.   You don't want to talk with me?

VINCENT.   You don't want to talk with me.

TERRY.   Because you're interfering in an official investigation

VINCENT.   That you need me to solve

TERRY.   So, the circle finishes the 360.

VINCENT.   Closer to 180.

TERRY.   See, Doctor. He's determined to be a detriment to the safety of society.

VINCENT. Can you be any less serious? I'm the hope of society.

TERRY. And a messiah complex. Doctor, are you taking notes?

USHA. Detective . . .

VINCENT. It's all right, Doctor. Her focus is askew. It's bad reception.

USHA. Vincent . . .

VINCENT. Detective Tolson, I am NOT your enemy. Not in the slightest.

TERRY. You're not my friend.

VINCENT. I never claimed to be your friend.

TERRY. And you're not my savior.

VINCENT. Not in the spiritual sense

TERRY. Not in any sense

USHA. This is counterproductive.

TERRY and VINCENT. No, it's productive.

USHA. I don't believe this.

VINCENT. There is a killer loose in this city.

TERRY. That we suspect.

VINCENT. That we know.

TERRY. And you're making things worse. Whatever and whoever's out there, you're putting this entire city in danger.

VINCENT. (*quickly*) By trying to protect myself, to protect you.

TERRY. Protect me? What?

USHA. Vincent, what are you talking about?

VINCENT. I've said enough.

TERRY. What did you say? What do you know?

VINCENT. I know you're up against a force unlike anything you've dealt with before.

TERRY. And there's a danger for us that you know about? Withholding any credible evidence from the authorities will get you in a large amount of trouble, Vincent.

VINCENT. I'm not withholding anything. It's induction.

TERRY. What does that even mean? How are you in danger? How are you?

USHA.   Vincent, is there something that you need to tell us?

VINCENT.   Doctor, there is nothing that I need to share with anyone. What I need is to be free, since I'm guilty of no wrong doing, and to be allowed to do my own research.

TERRY.   Not if it puts any of us in danger.

VINCENT.   *(raising his voice)* You're already in danger!

TERRY.   How?

VINCENT.   *(quickly)* How can you legitimately not know? The world is changing. Getting smaller and smaller. And there are forces that don't like people like you and me, people who are offended that someone cares about order, about protection, about doing the right thing in a wrong world. We're in an ever-speeding spiral of chaos, Detective. A web of nothingness and sorrow into which the spiders of hate and deceit climb into and make themselves at home. You're in their way. I'm in their way. Our very nature clashes with theirs. Yes, you and I are at 180, but for the sake of our very lives, we'd better find ourselves at a 360, or we won't survive.

TERRY.   What do you know?

USHA.   Detective, you need him.

TERRY.   What?

USHA.   You're the crazy one if you think this man's against you.

TERRY.   What do you know, Vincent?

VINCENT.   Detective, you arrested Greg Argaletti. As a result, the supply chain from Los Angeles was significantly disrupted. Then, less than twenty-four hours later, one of your sergeants brought you information that led to the arrest of Coco Davis. All it took was three hours to find that Minkley was working with him. Arrest. Arrest. Money stopped. Seven warehouses in Vegas, Reno, and Salt Lake scattered like roaches in daylight. Out. Gone. Calls. Messages. Someone must have suspected Hank Vidden, someone must have THREATENED Hank Vidden, because he turned himself into the FBI at a Walmart parking lot in Fargo six hours later. Then when they figured out they'd falsely accused Vidden, he ended up dead in FBI custody the next morning. No signs of struggle. Just a clean knife wound right through the chest. The natives are restless and putting the puzzle together. And they know how it fits—or soon will. *(pause)* And yesterday, you arrested Bobby Monday Finley.

TERRY.   How do you know all this?

USHA.   Monday?

VINCENT.   Immaterial. I just do. Like a whirlwind. And you made the first arrest, and now Finley.

USHA.   That's amazing. You are herby released. *(to Terry)* Hire him.

TERRY.   And I've arrested two of the key players in . . . *(figuring it out)*

VINCENT.   Yes . . . *(leading him)*

USHA.   Yes?

TERRY.   And it all leads back to . . . him.

USHA.   Who?

TERRY and VINCENT.   Xavier.

USHA.   Xavier?

TERRY.   Xavier.

VINCENT.   . . . who's putting the final pieces in the puzzle now.

TERRY.   And who wants me dead because of it all.

VINCENT.   Jigsaw piece.

TERRY.   But why would he want you dead?

VINCENT.   Who do you think your sergeant talked to?

TERRY.   What?

VINCENT.   And I *might* have gone to Salt Lake three nights ago to see exactly what was happening.

TERRY.   Vincent, how do you . . . do these things?

VINCENT.   How?

TERRY.   No, I'm beyond how. Just why?

VINCENT.   I don't know. I just do. It's just . . . whatever.

USHA.   Did you hear me? You've been free to go. You're not a prisoner here. Go protect yourself.

VINCENT.   Thank you for the emancipation, Dr. Ullman. But I've not been prisoner to be released. I've been a willing guest enjoying the hospitality of your facilities.

TERRY.   Then why are you still here? Why did you tell me all this? You never share this kind of information.

VINCENT.	Because I've been waiting here long enough and keeping you here with me long enough for us to spend some time together, in the same room, in the same place, at the same time.
TERRY.	What?
USHA.	But that's not wise if both of you are on this guy's . . .
TERRY.	Wait a minute. What? We're in the same place for . . .
VINCENT.	Let's call it convenience and opportunity.
TERRY.	You used me.
VINCENT.	You were trying to hold me for no reason.
TERRY.	Because you . . . forget it.
VINCENT.	I'm afraid it may now be too late, Detective.
TERRY.	What you do mean?
XAVIER.	*(enters, dressed at an orderly)* Vincent is right, as usual, Detective.
TERRY.	What? Who are you?
USHA.	What's your name? I don't recognize you.
XAVIER.	Doctor, I don't blame *you* for not recognizing me. I'm a bit beyond your range of expertise and knowledge. But Detective Tolson, tsk, tsk. Surely *you* haven't forgotten me already?
VINCENT.	Detective?
TERRY.	Xavier.
XAVIER.	Ah, age hasn't robbed you of your senses quite yet. Maybe the eyes are the first to go. Maybe not. Do not reach for your gun, Detective, and don't try to contact your subordinates. I have a trained marksman with his sights on the pretty little noggin of Dr. Ullman here. And anyway, it's not her life I'm interested in taking. It's a couple of flies in the ointment who are causing all sorts of trouble, trouble that can be easier solved by a flyswatter.
TERRY.	You don't have to do this. Let Dr. Ullman go.
XAVIER.	And void my life insurance policy? I haven't survived this business for this long by being stupid. This is between you and me—and between your P.I. boy Vincent and me. When my business is done, she goes safe. And I fade back into my, what did you call it, Vincent, my spider web of nothingness?
VINCENT.	We must be special, to warrant a visit from Xavier himself.

XAVIER. Very.

VINCENT. Like Hank Vidden?

XAVIER. Why do you think I brought this? (*He pulls out a long blade.*)

TERRY. In a hospital? Right here? Are you serious?

XAVIER. What better place? In an FBI safe house? A Wall Street executive washroom? The judge's chamber of a courtroom? All have worked. This will, too. It's good to get out and take care of things myself.

VINCENT. You have a dark mind, Xavier.

XAVIER. You're one to talk, Vincent. Are sure you don't want to switch teams? It's a bit more fun over here.

VINCENT. The benefits are short-lived.

XAVIER. For a mind of such capabilities, you fail to use logic. Look here. See where you are? See this knife. Do you know how many people I've killed with this blade?

VINCENT. Whatever the number, it's as high as it's going to go.

TERRY. What?

VINCENT. He's not going to kill us.

XAVIER. (*laughs*) Oh, yes I am.

VINCENT. No, you're not. You're not going to kill anyone else ever again.

XAVIER. You're delusional. Look around you. Look. Here. What do you see, Vincent?

VINCENT. You're not looking around *you*. Here in this room are two people whom you need dead. In the same room. At the same time. Coincidence? And I didn't come quietly to the ward. An ambulance was sent after me. A big commotion. An absolute spectacle. Followed by Detective Tolson conveniently coming here as well. I don't deal with Tolson. I don't particularly like the Detective. But here is Detective Tolson. When was the last time we talked in person?

TERRY. Before today?

VINCENT. Yes?

TERRY. Six, seven months ago, briefly.

VINCENT. Yet here we are today. I've been free to go. I haven't. I've waited. I never tell the fine details of what I've thinking. And I still haven't. However, I just shared with Detective Tolson, Dr. Ullman, and even you bits and pieces of information concerning how your apple cart has been recently overturned. And here you are in this hospital right when we are both here together.

XAVIER.   But you're overlooking two important things. A gun pointed at this pretty little head and a blade that's going to rip you up and out all over this floor.

VINCENT.   Well, no and . . . no. First, your driver and his companion were arrested two and a half minutes ago by four officers I tipped off when I first started talking with Detective Tolson. You see, I have a communication device known as a "cell phone," a device that can be used and remain hidden. And I have contacts that answer my calls and messages. Second, your marksman has already been taken out by one Sergeant Wayne Wentworth, the same detective whose services I used to get information to Detective Tolson concerning the needed arrest of Coco Davis, your friend, colleague, and if I'm not mistaken, brother of your current romantic companion, Francesca Davis. All that was worked out and taken care of.

XAVIER.   Clever, but not over. A knife can kill more brutally than a gun, and I can be out of here before anyone can test for your vitals.

VINCENT.   Which leads me to the last bit. I had everything else planned, but in here, this moment, I hadn't had time to plan.

TERRY.   What?

VINCENT.   Calm down, Detective. It's not over.

XAVIER.   But it's about to be.

VINCENT.   Yes, but not in the way you assume.

XAVIER.   Enlighten me.

VINCENT.   Gladly. This part is a bit of luck, pure luck.

TERRY.   What?

VINCENT.   When I knew we'd be in the same quarters, here in the hospital, I assumed it would just the three of us, that the detective and I would have to find some way to jump you, incapacitate you, but I didn't expect Dr. Ullman.

XAVIER.   Poor Dr. Ullman. She seems doomed to share the same fate as the two of you. I don't think you know who you're dealing with.

VINCENT.   See. You pass right over it. You're not looking. (*pauses*) Dr. Ullman?

USHA.   (*smiling, knowing what he's leading to*) Yes, Vincent.

VINCENT.   Where did you complete your medical degree?

USHA.   Johns Hopkins.

VINCENT.   And before that?

USHA.   Harvard Medical.

VINCENT.   And before that?

XAVIER.   She's a well-educated woman. (*sarcastically*) Kudos.

USHA.   Sackler School of Medicine, the University of Tel Aviv.

TERRY.   Which means you're Israeli.

XAVIER.   So.

VINCENT.   Israeli.

TERRY.   Israeli-educated. Which means you were a member of the . . .

USHA.   Israeli Defense Forces.

USHA punches XAVIER in the throat, disabling him, and making him drop the knife, which Terry immediately picks up. XAVIER is on the floor moaning and coughing when WAYNE, a police officer, walks in.

WAYNE.   Vincent, we . . . (*notices Terry and then Xavier on the floor*) . . . (*sheepishly*) Oh.

TERRY.   It's okay, Wentworth. I know. And it's okay . . . for now. Arrest this man. (*indicating Xavier*)

WAYNE.   (*cuffing and lifting a weak Xavier*) I have a . . . man with a gun, handcuffed, taken downstairs to the car, along with a couple of suspects from the parking lot.

TERRY.   We know.

WAYNE.   You do?

TERRY.   Yes, we have our sources. (*looking at Vincent*)

VINCENT.   (*to Usha*) You okay?

USHA.   I'm fine.

TERRY.   (*to Usha*) Do you realize what you've just done?

USHA.   Oh, I realize. My.

TERRY.   And you have no idea that you . . .

USHA.   Not as part of what needed to be done . . . until it clicked.

VINCENT.   I knew.

TERRY.   You had to figure it out.

VINCENT   I still knew. Just a reminder, Dr. Ullman. Good job.

USHA.   I've dedicated my life to saving lives . . .

TERRY.   And you continued that legacy today. More than you know. Get him out of here, Wentworth.

WAYNE.   Yes, ma'am. *(leaves with Xavier)*

USHA.   What now?

TERRY.   You ought to consider going home for the rest of the day, really the week. And Vincent, you need to go home, too.

VINCENT.   I'm sure they're not through with you.

TERRY.   You mean us.

VINCENT.   Yeah, us.

TERRY.   We'll keep a closer watch. Want to come and see me in my office after lunch tomorrow? We have a lot to discuss.

VINCENT.   I can do that.

TERRY.   We have some plans to make. Maybe we can avoid a few tragedies, save a few lives—with a little of your luck.

All three exit slowly.

Short Play 8/Scene 8—
Luck of the Draw

Four people are sitting around, talking casually.

BRADY.   And then (*laughing*) . . . and then she looked up and said, "Sir, I asked for a glass
           of water, not a waiter."

Everyone (BRADY, ANNA, YVETTE, and ZED) fall out laughing.

ZED.   Water! (*Laughing*)

YVETTE.   That's precious, Brady.

ZED.   Water!!

ANNA.   Calm down, Zed. You're encouraging him.

ZED.   I can't help it. It's funny.

BRADY.   It is, isn't it? I can't take credit, though. Ralph Hopper told me that one.

ZED.   Ralph?

YVETTE.   Ralph Hopper with the red nose?

ZED.   I didn't think he had a funny bone in his body.

BRADY.   Well, he told a good joke.

ANNA.   Maybe you're just the master joke teller that can redeem the dying word. (*kisses
           him on the forehead*)

YVETTE.   That'd be a great name for a short story, Anna. Can I steal it?

ANNA.   "The Master Joke Teller That Can Redeem the Dying Word"? Really?

YVETTE.   No, not all of it. Just "Redeem the Dying Word." Or some variation. I really
           have a headache. I can't concentrate tonight.

ZED.   You're probably dehydrated. You don't drink enough water.

YVETTE.   Here we go again.

ZED.   Am I right?

YVETTE.   Zed.

ZED.   Am I right?

YVETTE.   It doesn't matter.

ZED.   It always matters. *(to Brady)* It always matters.

ANNA.   Remember Dr. Baybrough in that writing class in Harper Hall, Freshman year?

YVETTE.   How could I forget him? He . . . *(realizing)* RED nose!

ANNA.   Yes. Isn't that crazy?

BRADY.   He couldn't help it. He has Rosacea or something.

ZED.   He was kinda mean, though.

BRADY.   Because he expected work to be turned in on time? He was a nice guy.

ZED.   You're just being touchy. You're turning into a stickler, too? Give those poor kids a chance to be kids.

ANNA.   He gives them plenty chances. He's an ol' softy. A pushover.

BRADY.   I am not a pushover. I just . . . understand people. At least I try.

ANNA.   I know. You're a sweetheart. That's why we love you so much.

YVETTE.   I *do* think I'm going to get something to drink. I don't like to admit it, but my husband is right. I don't drink enough water. Husband? That still doesn't sound right.

ZED.   What?

YVETTE.   No, I don't mean it sounds wrong. It just sounds so new. I'm not used to it.

ZED.   Well, "wife" sounds good to me. Or "wifey."

YVETTE.   If you say that again, I'm filing divorce papers.

ZED grins from ear to ear and then kisses YVETTE on the cheek.

YVETTE.   What do I see in that man?

ANNA.   Looks. Smarts. Good taste in friends.

YVETTE.   True. (pauses) I'm going to make some lemonade. Anybody want some?

ZED.   Lemonade? Where'd that come from?

YVETTE.   I'm tired of everything else. Hey, it's wet. And it hydrates.

ZED.   Sure.

BRADY.   I'm game.

ANNA.   I'll come help. You can tell what it's like to be a *wifey*.

YVETTE slaps her on the arm. She and ANNA exit to the kitchen.

ZED.	So.

BRADY.	What?

ZED.	So?

BRADY.	What? What's up?

ZED.	Nothing. What's up with you? (*grinning*)

BRADY.	You're freaking me out. (*pause*) Just . . . waiting. Thirsty for lemonade now. (*pause*) What?

ZED.	You know you need to do it?

BRADY.	What?

ZED.	You know?

BRADY.	What?

ZED.	Ask her to marry you.

BRADY.	WHAT?

ZED.	Ask her to . . .

BRADY.	(*Interrupting*) SHHH! What are you talking about? We're not even dating. We're not . . . a thing.

ZED.	Yes, you are.

BRADY.	 No, we're not. Are you dreaming all this up? Anna and I are friends.

ZED.	You love her.

BRADY.	Of course, I love her. She's my friend.

ZED.	No, you LOVE her.

BRADY.	I love you, and I love Yvette.

ZED.	Not like you love Anna.

BRADY.	What are you now, the love guru?

ZED.	No, I'm your friend.

BRADY.	Whom I love.

ZED.	Not in the same way.

BRADY.	You're crazy. Have you been drinking?

ZED.	It's time you settle down. Brady, you're my bud, my friend for years and years. Time's racing by. Right in there is Anna, ANNA, Brady! Anna! She adores you. And you love *her*. You've been putting this off and putting this off. You have to face facts and tell her how you feel.
BRADY.	And you know how I feel?
ZED.	I do.
BRADY.	You do?
ZED.	I do.
BRADY.	And how do you presume to know all this?
ZED.	Because I love *you*. You're my friend. And sometimes a friend has to step in to help.
BRADY.	You're impossible.
ZED.	I'm right.
BRADY.	You're stepping on ground that . . .
ZED.	I'm right.
BRADY.	I've always been . . .
ZED.	I'm right. And you know it. Someone has to step in and save you from your own mind.
BRADY.	I . . . Zed, I . . .
ZED.	Brady, it's Anna.
BRADY.	I . . . I can't.
ZED.	Because?
BRADY.	Because . . . she might not feel the same way. She may say, "That's not the kind of love I feel for you." You know: rejection.
ZED.	Worth a risk.
BRADY.	To lose a friendship?
ZED.	For love? For future family? Yes.
BRADY.	(*nervous*) I . . . I . . . You know you make a compelling argument.
ZED.	Law degree.
BRADY.	I hate you.

ZED.   I love you, too.

BRADY.   I have to get the courage. Maybe one day.

ZED.   There's no time like the present.

BRADY.   What? No. NO!

ZED.   Well, tomorrow then. Time's a wasting. You have years to live. You have
            children to father. You gotta get cracking. Anna loves you. You love her. Let
            her know. Take a risk.

BRADY.   I don't have everything together. I'm not independently wealthy. For Heaven's
            sake, I'm a school teacher.

ZED.   Noble. Bonus points. Caring. High school. Double bonus points. They're
            heathen. Make that triple. The love dial is creeping up.

BRADY.   Maybe one day.

ZED.   Tomorrow.

BRADY.   Not tomorrow. I don't have the words.

ZED.   You're a teacher. You always have the words. You're a writer. You float down
            rivers of words.

YVETTE.   (*from the kitchen*) You boys like it tart?

ZED.   Oh, yeah. The tarter the better. (*back to Brady*) You need to tell her. Life's too
            short. Let's do this. (*taking out a deck of cards*) We draw. You get the higher
            card, you take a few weeks to prepare, and then you tell her. I get the higher card,
            you tell her tomorrow, and I get to be best man.

BRADY.   But . . .

ZED.   Not your brother, not Charlie Mitchell, not Ralph Hopper. Me.

BRADY.   Why would I draw?

ZED.   Because you want to. And because you hope with everything within you that I
            get the higher card. Ready?

BRADY.   I . . .

ZED.   Ready?

BRADY.   Yes.

They draw. From the looks on their faces, it's evident that ZED wins.

ZED.   So, tomorrow it is.

BRADY.   I suppose. I'm a man of my word. (*getting bolder, stronger*)

ZED.   That you are. Now you have to figure out what to say.

BRADY.   Oh, I have it. I wrote it a long time ago.

ZED.   Why does that not surprise me?

BRADY walks out to the front of the stage and speaks over the audience.

BRADY.   I'm your "best" friend. I look out for you. I care about you so much that I'm honest with you about everything. And have to tell you . . . the truth. I know that you and I have been through a lot together. We've known each other a very long time. And I know you think that what we have is more than, well, friendship. Hear me out. Please. I love you very much.

YVETTE and ANNA walk in with a pitcher of lemonade and glasses.

YVETTE.   Lemonade's ready.

ANNA.   (*to Zed*) Oh, are those playing cards?

ZED.   Yeah. You guys want to play a game of luck?

Curtain closes.

Lowery Christopher Collins (Chris) has been an educator and writer for over thirty years. He is currently a professor of English at Panola College in Carthage, Texas. He has taught at the high school, middle school, and elementary school levels and as an English and literature instructor at the college and university level. For several years, he was a high school theatre director and a gifted education consultant. He's been honored with several teaching awards, including the Young Audiences of Northeast Texas Outstanding Service to the Profession Award and the Kennedy Center's Steven Sondheim Award for being one of the most "Inspirational Teachers" in the U.S.

He is also an award-winning playwright of over thirty scripts, a weekly newspaper columnist, a short story writer, a poet, a pianist, a vocalist, a songwriter, a recording artist with Daywind Studios, the founder and artistic director of Stagelands Theatre Company, an aspiring novelist, and a (former) choir director. He's taught a variety of classes, from rhetoric and composition to literature to acting to the Bible.

He holds a Bachelor of Arts Degree in English and History and a Master of Arts Degree in English from Stephen F. Austin State University in Texas and has served on fine arts and gifted education committees as well as on a board of governors for a small playhouse.

In addition to his interests in teaching, directing, and writing, he has a fondness for lighthouses, windmills, filmmaking, salsa, sculpture, Flannery O'Connor, travel, dominos, guacamole, social media, genetics, Maine, landscaping, pillows, gospel music, Shakespeare, marbles, YouTube, quantum physics, movies, weird jokes, maps, trees, cold rooms, and Texas.

 He can be reached at mrchriscollins@hotmail.com,

on Facebook at www.facebook.com/tofferdreams,

on Twitter at "tofferdreams,"

and at his website: www.ChristopherCollinsOnline.com.

To view Christopher Collins's books and other writing, visit Ponderlake Publishing, at www.ponderlake.com.